THIS BOOK BELONGS TO....*Michael Mee*..............

Xmas 1989
With Love,
Aunt Jackie.

ILUSTRACIONES: IBAÑEZ
ADAPTACION DE TEXTOS: ISABEL URUEÑA
GRAFISMO: JUAN FRANCISCO RAMOS

COPYRIGHT 1984 INTEREDICIONES J. M.
PUBLISHED BY PETER HADDOCK LTD
BRIDLINGTON, ENGLAND
PRINTED IN USSR

MY GIANT BOOK
OF
FAIRY STORIES

GULLIVER IN LILLIPUT

MY name is Gulliver and I am a doctor. One day, not very long ago, I decided to work as a doctor to a ship's crew because there was not much money to be earned in my small surgery and I have a family to look after.

This was not the first time I had travelled. When I was young and before I was married, I made several long trips—I love the sea.

But one day there was a heavy storm and we were shipwrecked. I grabbed hold of a plank and very quickly lost sight of the ship which was sinking. I think I was the only survivor.

After several hours of being cold and hungry, I saw a beach in the distance and swam to it. I fell asleep there because I was so tired.

When I woke up I tried to get up, but I couldn't! Hundreds of small ropes were holding me to the ground. All around me there were tiny people, armed with bows and arrows.

I tried talking to them in all the different languages

which I know—and that is a great many—but they were talking in a language that I couldn't understand. What was I going to do?

By pulling with all my force I managed to free my left arm and by making signs and putting my finger in my mouth I managed to let them know that I was hungry.

So they brought me 80 baskets of meat and 10 barrels of lovely wine. Some pieces of the meat were almost like birds' feet but when I had finished it all I felt much better.

I fell asleep again straight away. I think they must have mixed a sleeping drug into the wine. When I woke up I found myself on a huge moving platform, taking me to the city.

They were certainly a very clever race of people. They had done a lot of work while I was asleep.

"I must convince them that I don't want to hurt them," I said to myself. They left me at the door of a building which they had given me to live in. It was an ancient temple which was no longer used.

Everyone, including the Royalty, came to see me, but nobody was very brave towards me.

Finally I convinced them that I came in peace. The King ordered his teachers to teach me their language and everybody started getting used to me. They were no longer frightened of me, although they would not unfasten my chains, even at night.

As soon as I could understand them they taught me their laws and customs. They were an interesting race of people.

One day the King's Prime Minister came to see me and read me a paper which I had to sign and then the King would release me.

"You must help us fight our enemies who want to invade us."

"You have been so kind to me that I promise to defend you in an attack," I replied.

"One of my brothers is King of that island, but I have fallen out with him. His ship is in the harbour ready to invade us. Can we destroy it?" the King asked me.

"Certainly, your Majesty. I shall do it straight away to stop the invasion."

That night I collected the strongest ropes I could find. In the morning I went to the island of Blufescu and tied up the ships and towed them to Lilliput.

The sailors were terrified by my size and swam to the shore so no violence was necessary. This pleased me because I had nothing against them.

The capture of the enemy's ships was a very celebrated event, but not everybody was happy. A nobleman whose life I had saved one day, told me that people were conspiring against me.

"They are trying to convince the King that you should be killed because you did not destroy all the people from Blufesco. They are saying that you are a traitor."

I did not think much of that! That very afternoon I took the ships which I had stolen and went to the neighbouring King, telling him that I was a peace-loving person.

"Then join us, if you like," said the King of Blufescu. "My brother lied to you. I don't want to fight with him nor do I have any desire to rule Lilliput."

So I lived there peacefully. The tiny
inhabitants of Blufescu were much more
friendly than those of Lilliput and much
more peaceful.

One day some sailors came running to me
telling me about a large object they had seen
in the sea.

Nothing could have surprised me more than to see this object was a ship which the sea had brought for me! I asked the King of Blufescu to help me and started to prepare it.

Five hundred women sewed sails the size I asked for, and soon the ship was ready to sail.

I was sad to leave my friends, but I longed to get home.

Loaded with food and livestock that they had given me, I took to the sea, trusting in luck.

Several days went by until one afternoon I saw a sail on the horizon. I waved my shirt, made signs, unfolded the sails of my ship and finally managed to make them see me.

It was an English ship which picked me up and took me home.

I told them all about my incredible adventure. Nobody would have believed me unless they had seen the tiny animals which I had brought with me. Thanks to them, fortune was to smile on me always, since I have earned a lot of money by showing them throughout England and by writing my memoirs. Since that day I have lived comfortably with my family, although sometimes I would like to travel and have adventures again.

THE END

THE PIPER OF HAMELIN

ONCE upon a time, in a village called
Hamelin, something happened which the
people who live there have never forgotten.

Hamelin was a very prosperous town. The
people worked leather and silver very well
and earned a lot of money. They had only
one fault—they were a bit greedy.

The Mayor of Hamelin was the most greedy person in the town. As soon as Spring arrived he would not wear socks, so as not to wear them out!

"It is better not to spend what you can save," was his motto.

But one day everybody was very worried because a terrible plague was destroying the people—the rats.

The rats were terrible. They ate all the cheese that the shop-keeper had. They ate the lace in the general store. There were no books left in the school.

Everyone was talking about these disasters in the town saying:
"Down with the rats. They must go."

"Yes, but how are we going to get rid of them?" asked somebody.

Then Mr Samuel, who was the oldest person in the place, spoke:

"There is a man who can do it," he said. "He is a kind of magician who, using a flute, can get rid of any plague. I could write to him, if you like."

"Write, write," everyone shouted.

A letter was sent straight away and it soon reached its destination. The Piper read it very carefully.

"They need me in Hamelin," he murmured. "I must go there then, if that is what they want."

And the very next day, without further thought, he set off for Hamelin with his magic flute under his arm.

When he reached the town he spoke to the Mayor.

"It is terrible," he told him, "the rats won't leave us alone. You must do something."

"I shall deal with them," replied the Piper.

"In exchange I shall
ask for seven gold coins
and seventy silver coins,
when the rats have
gone."

"That sounds quite
dear to me," said the
Mayor. "But if there is
no other solution, we will
pay what you ask."

Once the price for his work had been agreed, the Piper went off up the road, took out his magic flute and started playing.

What lovely music. The people came to the windows and clapped as he went past. Nobody had ever heard anything as lovely. Not even the organist in the church could play that well.

But the rats loved the sound the most. They left what they were doing and ran out through all the doors, sewers, over the walls—it was as if they couldn't resist it. The Piper's music attracted them like a magnet attracts nails.

After a while, hundreds and thousands of rats were following the magician through the streets of Hamelin.

The clever Piper was playing and playing, all along the road, getting nearer and nearer the river which ran on the outskirts of the town. He went into the water and all the rats

which were following him went into the water too, and instantly drowned.

"No more rats in Hamelin," thought the Piper as he returned to the town.

The people cheered as he returned. But when it was time to pay, things got nasty. The Mayor did not want to pay him.

"In fact, all you have done is play your flute," he said. "That doesn't seem like very

hard work to me. I'll give you one gold coin and even that is more than you deserve."

"I don't want your money," replied the very angry Piper. "You'll pay for your greed in full!" he exclaimed.

The Piper started playing his magic flute
again, but this time he played a different
tune, softer and more light-hearted than the
tune he has used to attract the rats. They had
wanted to dance and jump about, being able
to think only about the lovely music.

But this time all the boys and girls in the town felt like this. As soon as they heard the first part of the tune they started dancing after the Piper, and just like the rats, they could not stop.

"Peter! Angela!" called their mothers.

But it was in vain—the children seemed to have gone deaf.

They could hear only the music which was dragging them along behind the Piper.

And soon the town was left without any children!

"What are we going to do without our sons?" they asked one another.

"Nothing will be the same without them," others cried.

"Mayor," they all said, "tell us what we can do to get our children back to the town."

"I don't know," replied the Mayor. "I just don't know." But he knew that this was the Piper's revenge.

Then the Piper appeared and said to the Mayor, "This is your fault. You tried to cheat me, saying that all I had done was to play my flute. Well, if you think it is so easy, you get the children back to town and I shall not bother with the money you owe me."

"Has this terrible thing happened to us because you wanted to avoid paying this man?" cried the Mayor's wife, who was there.

"But, dear wife, I was only trying to save some of the town's money," murmured the Mayor.

"And look what has happened because of your saving," screamed the Mayoress, who was very angry by now. "You will pay the Piper everything you promised him immediately."

Once he had collected what was rightfully his, the Piper set off for the mountain again, playing his magic flute.

And so all the children of Hamelin returned to their homes safe and sound. As for the Mayor and Mayoress, they will never forget the lesson that the Piper taught them and will never be greedy again.

In colours bright and colours pale, we bring an end to this our tale.

THE END

DONKEY'S HIDE

A long time ago there was a kingdom where a King and his wife ruled very happily. They did not want for anything nor could they be happier and their subjects adored them for their kindness.

Their greatest joy was their little daughter.

"We have only one daughter," they said to one another, "but she is so pretty and good that we don't need another."

But one day the Queen became ill and
none of the doctors knew how to cure her. If
they couldn't find a cure she would surely die.
Before she died, however, she said to the
King:

"Promise me that you will marry
only a woman who is more beautiful and
better than I am, and I will die happy."
The King, full of grief, promised her
this without thinking, although he never
wanted to marry again.

And so the Queen died and the King spent several years without anyone being able to console him.

His ministers tried to convince him that he should seek a wife, but the King asked them:

"Who could possibly be better and more beautiful than my first wife?"

But one day he realized that his daughter had grown into a beautiful

princess and he decided
to marry her, without
thinking that it was
madness.

The frightened Princess
went to see the fairy
godmother and told her
what had happened.

"My father has gone
mad! What can I do?"

"If you do what I tell
you, you will be freed
from this dreadful
wedding," said the fairy.

"Tell him that, as a condition to this wedding, you must have a dress the colour of the weather—I don't think he can get that!"

So the Princess did just that, but the King found a dress-maker who made a beautiful dress with all the colours of the blue sky, the white clouds and the fine afternoon breeze. He was very determined to marry his daughter.

So the Princess said, just like the fairy had told her to:

"That's lovely but now I should like a dress the colour of the moon. If you cannot give me this, then I shall not marry you."

But once again the King managed to get the dress his daughter wanted, a dressmaker

made it the colour of the moon.

Again the Princess was frightened and did what the fairy had told her to do. She put another condition to her father:

"I would like one more thing—a dress the colour of the sun—no less bright, mind you."

Once again the King went away. He found another dress-maker capable of making a dress as bright as the sun.

"And now my final condition," said the Princess, just like the fairy had told her to. "I want you to give me the hide of the magical donkey which you have in the stables. The one which gives out gold from its mouth when it brays!"

Now the King liked the donkey very much—it was a source of wealth for his

kingdom—but he would kill it to give the hide to his daughter.

"What shall I do now?" the Princess asked the fairy.

"There is no alternative but for you to escape," she replied.

"Disguise yourself as a beggar with the donkey's hide. I will make sure that your box of clothes is sent after you without anybody knowing."

So that is just what the Princess did. She dressed as a beggar with the donkey's hide on her back so that nobody in the palace would

recognize her. Her box of clothes followed her, invisible to everyone, just as the fairy had said it would be.

"Perhaps my father will forget his wild intentions one day so that I can return," she said.

After several weeks she reached another kingdom and asked for work in the palace kitchen. They needed a scullery maid, so they let her in, and the Princess, who everyone started calling Donkey's Hide, scrubbed all day long without resting, but she was very happy.

The other women servants mocked her without knowing that she was of very good birth. But the Princess put up with it all.

Only on Sundays was she able to rest. Then she would shut herself in her room and try on the royal clothes that her father had given her so that she could feel like the Princess that she really was.

But one day the Prince happened to be passing in the passage-way and the door was slightly open. When he saw her he fell helplessly in love with her.

The Prince asked everyone about her, but
they laughed, "Donkey's Hide is the most
ugly and dirty person in the palace," they
said. "You *must* be mistaken."

The young man was helplessly love-sick
and nothing could console him.

The doctors did not know what was the
matter and his parents sat at his bedside
weeping because they loved him so much.

The wise men of the kingdom said, "He
should get married."

One day the Prince said, "I would like a cake made by Donkey's Hide."
Now it was such a long time since he had asked for anything to eat that they decided to let him have this and asked the girl to

make a cake for the Prince. Donkey's Hide asked to be left alone in the kitchen and prepared a lovely cake. She dropped her most expensive ring in the middle of it.

The Prince ate the cake and found the ring.

"I shall marry the woman whom this ring fits," he said, much to the amazement of his parents.

Immediately all the ladies of the court were called, including those from neighbouring kingdoms, but the little ring was too small for all of them.

"No, not this one," said the Prince, to one after another.

Donkey's Hide entered while the Prince was seeking the owner of the ring. She was dressed in the richest of her real clothes. As soon as the young man saw her he recognized his love and the colour returned to his cheeks.

The ring fitted Donkey's Hide's delicate finger perfectly.

"This is the wife I want," said the Prince who was immediately better again.

So the wedding plans were made as quickly as possible. But the Princess could not be totally happy without seeing her father again so she sent for him.

On seeing his daughter, the King asked her to forgive him.

"I have wanted to see you for such a long time just to tell you that I must have been mad. I want you to be very happy."

And when they were friends again, the wedding took place and they all lived happily ever after.

THE END

JACK AND THE BEAN STALK

JACK and his mother were very poor. They had only a tiny vegetable garden and one cow which was called White Milk. But one day the cow stopped giving milk.

"What shall we do now, mother?" asked Jack.

"We have no choice but to sell her," replied his mother. "Take her to market and be careful that nobody tries to trick you."

So the boy set off along the road to the village. After a while he met a man who was going in the same direction.

"Where are you taking that cow, young man?" asked the man.

"I am going to sell her because she isn't giving milk any more," replied Jack.

"I will swap her for this little sack of seeds," said the man. "They are magical and you will make your fortune."

So Jack went home pleased with his magic beans. But his mother was very angry.

"You're useless," she grumbled. "What are we going to do now, without a cow or any money?"

"Mother, you will see that these beans will save us from our poverty," said Jack and he planted them in the vegetable garden without further ado.

During the night the plant grew and grew. These were magic beans indeed!"See, the man did not trick me," said Jack to his mother when they got up in the morning.

"Indeed, but how is this plant going to be any use to us? It hasn't got any flowers or fruit," replied his mother.

"I'm going to climb it and see what I can find," he said.

Jack climbed higher and higher and at the top there was a door.

"And who are you?" asked the woman who was standing there. "Don't you know that a terribly cruel person lives here?"

"No, I didn't," replied Jack, "but my mother and I have nothing to eat. Could you possibly give me something that we can live off?"

"Come in and
choose what you
like," said the
kind woman,
"but hurry because my husband may
come back."

Jack could not contain his astonishment
when he saw such riches.

"Is that human flesh I smell?" came the
terrifying voice of the ogre who had just come
home.

"No, there's nobody here," said the
woman, hiding Jack behind her skirt so that
the ogre could not see him.

Hidden by the ogre's wife, Jack managed to reach the bean stalk and hurried to climb down, homeward again. In his pocket was a handful of money which he had taken.

What a fright! He flew, feet first, sliding down the bean stalk in a spiral.

Jack and his mother lived quite happily without any money shortage until they had spent all the gold coins which the child had got from the giant's home.

"What are we going to do now?" cried his mother, when she saw that they had only one coin left.

"Don't worry mother," replied Jack. "Tomorrow I will go back to the ogre's house and see what I can find."

So, the following morning, Jack climbed up to the ogre's house and knocked on the door.

"Is that you again?" asked the woman. "My husband is sleeping so don't make any noise."

"I was wondering if you might give me some more gold because we have used up the coins you gave us," said the boy.

"Go and take what you want," she replied.

He was just picking up a
beautiful golden hen when
he heard the terrible voice
of the ogre shouting, "I
can smell flesh. Who's
there?"

"There's nobody here—you must have been
dreaming," replied his wife, hiding Jack in
the same way as before, until the child could
climb down the bean stalk with the golden
hen.

What a marvellous hen. Every day it laid an egg of pure gold. At last Jack and his mother would never be poor again. But the child said:

"Among the ogre's treasures I saw a lovely golden lyre which I should love to have."

"Don't be too ambitious," replied his mother. "With this hen we already have enough to live on, and richly too."

But Jack decided one day to climb up again for the golden lyre. He did not want it out of greed, but to have it to play in his spare time, because he was sure it would sound marvellous. However when he arrived the woman was surprised to see him. "You have come back again? My husband has found out that the hen is missing and he is very angry," she said.

"I only want the golden lyre. I promise I shan't come back again for anything else," begged Jack.

"Good," said the woman, "take it then"—she was very kind hearted.

However, just then the ogre appeared, having heard the noise.

"Ah, so it is you who is the thief," he roared. "Now you will get what you deserve—I'm going to eat you."

And he tried to finish Jack off with one blow.

But Jack ran very fast and managed to reach the bean stalk before the ogre could catch him. He started to climb down to his home, but the ogre was chasing him down the beanstalk.

"Stop, thief, I'm going to teach you a lesson," he shouted furiously.

When Jack heard the ogre's shouts his hair stood on end!

"Mother, Mother," he shrieked, "quickly bring the axe!"

Jack reached the bottom of the bean stalk first, and taking the axe which his mother had waiting for him, made two big cuts in the trunk of the magic plant.

Chop, chop – the trunk split and the ogre fell from a great height, killing him outright.

"I feel sorry for his wife – she was very kind to me," thought Jack, "but he nearly killed me."

"You see mother, the man was right, the plant has made our fortune," said Jack.

And he started playing the golden lyre. The notes were just as sweet as he had imagined them to be.

And from that day on thanks to the hen with the golden eggs, they were never poor again. And, although he was only small, Jack became famous with his golden lyre and lived happily ever after.

THE END

FEARLESS JACK

ONCE upon a time there was a man who had two sons. The elder was very hard working, but the younger one, whose name was Jack, did not want to hear any mention of learning a trade.

He said he had only one interest in life. "I

want to know what fear is and to learn to tremble. That is all I want."

So everybody thought he was mad.

One day Jack's father said to him, "We are not very rich, so if you don't want to work like your brother, you'll have to go out into the world and make a fortune."

So Jack left his family and went forth into the world, intending to learn about fear.

"I want to be able to tremble with fear," he said to himself.

He spent the night at an inn and told the inn-keeper, "I am looking for someone who can make me tremble with fear."

"Then you've come to the right place," replied the inn-keeper. "In this kingdom

there is an enchanted castle full of horrible creatures. Nobody escapes from there. The King has promised his daughter's hand to anyone who succeeds in spending three nights there."

The following day Jack went to see the King and said:

"Your Majesty, I should like to spend three nights in the enchanted castle and then marry the Princess."

The King took him to the gates of the sinister place.

"As you wish," replied the Monarch. "You seem like a brave young man. Good luck."

Once inside the castle Jack lit a fire and got ready for bed, as it was already late. Suddenly four enormous cats appeared and attacked him furiously.

"Get off! Get off!" shouted Jack. "Away with you you horrible creatures, you ought to learn some manners!"

He drove them away with a burning stick, and without further thought got ready for bed.

He had scarcely closed
his eyes when the bed
gave a mighty jerk, almost
as if it was alive, and
threw him to the ground.
   "Well, I have to sleep,
bed or no bed," said Jack
to himself, and he cuddled
down on the floor with a
rug near the fire. He slept
like a log throughout the
night with nothing to
disturb him.

At midnight on the
following night several
skeletons came down the

chimney, followed by a horrible figure of a man cut into two parts. "Hey you!" said Jack. "Stop fooling about and let's have a game of skittles. These skeletons will do!" They played skittles

with the skeletons' bones. Jack being very clever won the game.

"Now as my prize for winning, leave me to sleep quietly tonight," suggested Jack.

Hissing and shouting the man had no choice but to go so Jack was able to go to sleep.

The third night
had scarcely started
when Jack saw an
enormous giant
appear with an axe
and an anvil.

"I have come to
finish you off!"
roared the giant.

"We shall see," replied
Jack without even
thinking about it.

"What can you do?"

"You'll see," replied
the giant. "I'm going to
show you that I am
stronger than you are."

The giant placed the anvil in the middle of the room, took the axe and almost split the anvil in two with the first blow! What a blow!

"You saw that?" he said to Jack. "I don't think you could do that could you? So it would be easy for me to kill you."

"Well," said Jack, "I can do that with one hand!"

Jack grabbed the axe and said to the giant: "Come closer to the anvil so that you can see my blow more closely," and as the giant approached he swung the axe so that the giant's beard was buried in the slot which the giant himself had made!

"Help! Save me, save me," cried the giant.

"Good, now he won't stop me from sleeping like a log for the rest of the night."

And when the third night was over the castle seemed quite different. It was clean, shining and gave no cause for fear. Jack went to see the King and the Princess who were waiting for him.

"Splendid," said the King on seeing Jack. "You have disenchanted the castle with all its hazards. You will marry my daughter."

They had a wonderful wedding, the young couple seemed very happy. But Jack was sometimes sad.

"I still don't know what fear is. Even in the enchanted castle I didn't learn to tremble."

"What can I do to help you?" asked the Princess who loved him very much and wanted to see him happy all the time.

Now the nanny who had looked after the Princess was a truly good and wise woman. The girl confided in her a great deal and told her Jack's problem.

"What can I do to help him, nanny?" sighed the Princess.

"Don't cry my child. Do what I tell you and your husband will be freed from his problem forever," replied the nanny.

That night, following the nanny's advice, the Princess rose before dawn. With her golden jug she took some cold water from the garden fountain and some of the little fishes which lived there.

"If nanny is right this will free Jack from all his worries," she thought.

The Princess poured the contents of the jug all over Jack while he was still asleep so that he awoke with a fright!

"What are you doing wife?" he exclaimed. "What are you pouring all over me?"

From that day on Jack was completely happy and nobody could stop him because, thanks to the Princess, he had learned to tremble.

Now he knows exactly what it means to tremble.

THE END

RAPUNZEL

ONCE upon a time in a
far away country there
lived a King and Queen who very much
wanted a child. Finally, one day, the Queen
said to her husband, the King:

"Rejoice, husband, I am soon to become a
mother!"

The King jumped for joy. He organized
feasts and concerts. The whole kingdom was
awaiting the birth of the baby.

The Queen was very well but she wanted some unusual things. One morning she said to the King:

"I want a turnip salad from the witch's garden."

"But, my dear, we have our own turnips in the palace," replied the King.

But he could not convince her. It had to be those and only those. So the King had to carefully steal turnips from the garden of the kingdom's powerful witch.

The King was just creeping away when the witch appeared!

"Stop there!" she said. "You are the King, but *this* is *my* garden. Don't you know that I punish people who rob me very severely?"

"Oh please don't curse us," begged the King. "It was a fancy of my wife and I didn't want to deny her of it."

"I will let you go on condition that you give me the child which your wife is shortly to have," replied the witch.

The King saw no way other than to promise
this and so when the Princess was born they
called her Rapunzel and gave her to the
kingdom's witch. The witch who was kind if
you did not do anything against her, loved
Rapunzel and looked after her for three years
as if she were her own daughter. The child
loved her very much too.

However, when Rapunzel was three years old the witch began to worry that she would leave her so she locked her in a high tower without a door. The poor child was very bored and let her long tresses of hair hang out of the window so that the birds and butterflies could land on them.

"How lonely I am," sighed Rapunzel. "If only I could talk to someone."

One day a young Prince was passing by when he heard Rapunzel singing in her tower.

"What are you doing up there, young lady?" he asked.

Rapunzel told him that she lived there, guarded by the witch.

The Prince was so taken by her beauty that he fell in love with her and promised to visit her every afternoon.

The Prince kept his promise. Not a day went by without him visiting Rapunzel, making use of the witch's absence. He asked Rapunzel if she could come down to him so that he could see her more closely. "I can't," replied Rapunzel, "but you could climb up my tresses of hair."

So in this way they were able to be together for a short time every day.

One morning, when the witch came to give her her dinner, she said:

"Now I am old I can't see you very well, Rapunzel."

"If you want to see me more closely you can climb up my tresses, just like the Prince does," replied the young girl without thinking what she was saying.

"What Prince is this who climbs up your tresses?" roared the witch, enraged.

Rapunzel, who couldn't lie, told her the truth and, with every word she heard the witch got more and more angry, jealous of Rapunzel's love which she didn't

want to share with anybody. In her fury she took her magic wand and as she said some strange words Rapunzel felt the tower shaking. Everywhere there was a strange fire which did not burn.

Within seconds Rapunzel was carried through the air to a huge sandy desert.

"This is a punishment from my Aunt, the witch," wept the poor girl. "I shall never leave here nor return to see my dear Prince."

Then a crow appeared carrying food from the witch who did not want her to die from hunger.

The next day the Prince arrived at the tower and called to Rapunzel, but there was no reply.

"Call all you like, but your love will not appear," said the witch, laughing cruelly.

"What have you done with her?" asked the young man fearfully. The witch left without answering his question.

The young man tried to climb the high tower to see if Rapunzel was locked up in there. But there was a hawthorn bush which caught his eyes.

"Ouch, goodness me, I have gone blind," exclaimed the Prince.

And so it was; he fell to the ground, abandoning his climb and staggered about, hitting every stone, since he had lost his sight.

For seven long years the Prince wandered aimlessly from one end of the earth to the other, eating roots and fruit which fell from the trees. In the villages he begged for shelter. In the fields he slept under the trees.

"Ah, dear Rapunzel," he wailed, day and night. "Where are you? I shall never be able to see you again." Little by little the

Prince travelled hither
and thither, and one day
he crossed the desert
where poor Rapunzel
lived, abandoned by
everybody and fed by the
crows.

As soon as she saw the
Prince in the distance she
recognized him and ran
towards him.

"My dear Prince," said
Rapunzel, "don't you
recognize me?"

Then Rapunzel realized that the Prince did not recognize her because he was blind and she wept bitterly. Her tears fell on her dear Prince's eyes and he immediately regained his sight.

"My dear Rapunzel," he exclaimed joyfully, "I can see you again."

Having recovered his sight the Prince took Rapunzel back to her father's Kingdom. They found that the King had died and that everybody was looking for her to take the throne. So the Prince was crowned King and Rapunzel Queen, and they lived happily for many years to come.

THE END

THE HOUSE BY THE WOOD

A woodcutter who lived at the edge of the wood had a wife and three daughters. The woodcutter went to work every day to cut wood to sell in the nearby village. One day he said to his

wife, "Send our eldest daughter to the wood today with my dinner. It's about time she started to help us. I will scatter some grains of millet so that she can find me."

The young girl left the house at midday with the basket of food for her father, following the millet track. She soon lost her way however because the birds had eaten almost all the grain and the girl got quite lost. When she got hungry she ate what was in the basket and carried on walking. Finally she saw a light in the distance and went towards it.

The girl knocked at the door of the house and then went in. Inside there was an old man with his three animals which he was talking to as if they were people.

"I am lost, sir," said the girl. "Could I possibly spend the night here?"

"Well, my little animals, what do you say?" said the old man.

"Let her stay," exclaimed the three all at the same time.

"You may stay in exchange for preparing the supper," concluded the old man in a kind voice.

The girl prepared a rich soup from what she found in the larder. She laid the table and served supper for herself and the old man. When they had finished, the girl asked:

"Where can I sleep? I am so tired."

The old man took the girl upstairs where
she got ready to go to bed.

Meanwhile, the animals were singing:

"You've done yourself proud,
While we haven't fed,
Soon you will find
what we've done to your bed!"

The girl took no notice of the animals and fell asleep. Soon, however, the whole house started shaking and the floor opened up! What a terrible fright the girl had on waking up in the middle of that clamour. Then she fell, bed and all, through a hole.

When would she stop? In the cellar, to be imprisoned there!

The woodcutter and his family were very worried by the loss of their eldest daughter. "She must have fallen asleep in the wood. She'll soon come back," assured the father. "Send my dinner today with our second daughter. I will scatter lentils along the track so that she can find me and so that she doesn't get lost."

However, the birds ate the lentils and the second girl got lost too.

Just like her sister, she came at last to the old man's house, who suggested that she prepare the supper if she wished to spend the night there. The girl said yes.

As she was very clever she made a lovely meal and she and the old man ate with relish.

"May I go to bed now?" she asked. "I am
very tired after walking so far."

      "You have done yourself proud,
      While we haven't fed,
      Soon you will find
      what we've done to your bed!"
sang the animals while the girl got ready for
bed. She had not been asleep long when the
floor opened up and she fell into the cellar
where her sister had been imprisoned since
the previous day.

The following day it was the little one's turn to take the father's dinner. This time the man scattered peas, which were bigger, but the birds ate those up too, so the poor child got lost.

When night fell she saw the old man's house in the distance and went to it.

When she went into the house and asked if she might spend the night there, the old man suggested that she should prepare the supper in exchange for his hospitality.

The girl hastened to cook a lovely pie using what was in the larder.

Supper was soon ready. However, before eating, the girl said:

"I can't eat my supper without giving something to these poor animals," and so she prepared their favourite dishes, crumbs in milk for the chicken, corn for the hen and grass for the spotted cow.

Then she had supper herself with the old man and when they had finished she asked him to show her where she could sleep.

As soon as she lay down she fell asleep so she did not hear the animals in the house singing:

"With us you eat,
Us you serve,
A peaceful sleep
is what you deserve!"

She slept all night long but when dawn broke the house started to shudder from its very foundations and the girl awoke,

terrified. There seemed
to be an earthquake. The
walls were moving as
though they were
spinning. The ground
heaved, the bed seemed
to be breaking up. All
the commotion was not
for nothing, though. The
house changed into a
luxurious palace and her
humble room changed
into a lovely chamber, fit
for a Queen.

"Don't be afraid," said a fine Prince who was looking at her from the foot of the bed. "I am the old man for whom you prepared supper yesterday and

these servants were the three animals you looked after. Your kindness has freed us from a terrible spell."

And taking the girl, the Prince asked the woodcutter for her hand in marriage and the whole family went to live with the young couple in the palace. The two elder sisters came to understand their selfishness and never again forgot to care for animals.

Everyone lived happily ever after.

THE END

KING MIDAS

MIDAS was the king of a small Greek state.

One day while he was walking in the country he met a servant of the god Dionisius who had got lost and he took him back to his palace.

He looked after the servant for a week just like a friend, until he got better.

Then Midas went, with the servant, to see Dionisius.
"Thank you very much for what you have done for my servant ," said the god. "Tell me what you want and I shall grant it."

After thinking for a little while, Midas replied, "I would like everything I touch to turn to gold."

"So be it," replied Dionisius.

"It's true," he cried in astonishment. "It has changed to gold. I shall not have any more money problems in my small kingdom. From now on I shall be very rich."

Dionisius did not like Midas's request, but said nothing. When Midas

Midas tested this power in Dionisius's palace garden. He touched a hazel branch.

arrived back at his palace he went to open the door, and it changed to gold at a single touch.

"Marvellous," said Midas, very happily. "The god has fulfilled his promise."

The servants were amazed. They had never seen anything like it before!

As he was tired from his journey he asked for dinner to be served, but no sooner had he touched the food that it turned to gold!

"And how am I to eat if everything changes to gold when I touch it?" King Midas asked himself.
Soon he realized that he had made a terrible mistake in asking this favour from the god Dionisius.

125

Midas's wife, much as she loved him, did not come to kiss him for fear of being changed into a golden statue. Neither did his daughter come to see him as she would usually have done.

"How foolish I am," said Midas. And without thinking he touched his forehead and his face started to shine as if it were gold!

Midas, regretting his greed, went to the temple to ask forgiveness from the gods.
"How can I free myself from this curse?" he wept.

An old man appeared, who advised him:
"Go and find a fountain which is in the sacred mountains. Go there alone on foot. Wash your forehead in its water and you will be freed from the evil."

Midas travelled for several days before reaching the magic spring and, when he reached it, he washed himself in the crystalline water.

"I shall never be greedy again," he said, when he saw he was cured. "From now on I shall be a humble pilgrim and travel the world. I shall worship the gods and live in my palace only when my heart is pure again."

No sooner said than done. He travelled throughout Greece as a pilgrim for several years visiting all the temples which men had built to worship the gods.

When he considered that he had done sufficient penitence he decided to go home as his kingdom needed him to attend to affairs of state.

On reaching his kingdom, he came one day to a field where the god Apollo and the shepherd Pan were comparing their musical skills.

"I play my flute better than you play your lyre," said Pan, which was a very vain declaration. So Apollo decided that the people should be the judges.

However, when Apollo took up his lyre and started singing everybody was in ecstasy since it really was proper music. Everyone who was listening felt as if they were in heaven!

Firstly Pan played his flute. He played common melodies and was a bit out of tune. However, the people clapped as they were very polite.

There was no doubt about it and the jury said that Apollo was the winner. Midas however, who was very ignorant about music, since he had only worried about his money up to then, as we all know, said, in a very loud voice:

"I don't agree. I liked Pan's playing the most."
Ignorance is always very bold.
"Not only are you an ignoramus but you are insolent too!" roared Apollo who was very strict.
"You should have donkey's ears seeing as you are not ashamed of being a donkey!"

And after he said this, Midas's ears started growing and were covered with hair like those of an ass.

Just think of his misfortune! Midas knew that he had behaved like a fool. But he had to find a way to hide those enormous ears, so he let his hair grow so they could not be seen.

"I shall lose the respect of my subjects if they see my ears!" he thought.

Only his hair-dresser knew his terrible secret.

The god Apollo however wished the people to know what he had done to Midas, as a warning to ignorant people. Therefore he made the servant feel as if he just *had* to tell everyone.

And the servant could not contain himself. He went down to the river, dug a hole and told the earth that Midas had donkey's ears. After this he was satisfied.

But by the side of the river there was a bed of reeds and when the wind made the reeds move a murmuring could be heard which said:

"King Midas has donkey's ears. King Midas has donkey's ears."

And so everyone came to know about it just as Apollo had wanted.

Ignorance always brings misfortune and everyone should know that.

THE END

THE BRAVE TAILOR

ONCE upon a time there was a large kingdom and in the capital lived a young tailor who was hard working and skilful.

As he was only young he was not very well known and had only enough work to keep himself going.

"How I should like to be the King's tailor," he said to himself.

One warm summer afternoon a group of flies came into the tailor's workshop. They buzzed around him and would not let him work.

"Off, horrible flies!" cried the tailor, trying to drive them away. "You're distracting me and I *must* deliver this garment today."

As the tailor saw some of the flies settle on the wall, in the sun, he crept up on them and struck out suddenly with his fly swatter.
"Wallop! That'll teach you some manners!" he said.

The remaining flies hastened from the workshop which had suddenly become a dangerous place for them. They could no longer calmly loaf around there in the sun.

The tailor found, much to his surprise, that he had killed no less than seven flies with one blow.

"Eh," he said to himself, "I have killed seven in one go. That makes me a great fly exterminator. I must tell my neighbours about this straight away."

He ran out into the street crying joyfully, "I have killed seven, with one blow, I have killed seven!"

Folk gazed at him
astonished, because he
was only small and not
very well-built. As he had
not said *what* he had
killed everybody thought
he meant people, not
flies!

Rumour passed from mouth to mouth and finally reached the royal ears of His Majesty.

"One of your subjects is so strong that he killed seven with a single blow," declared the Prime Minister.

"Bring him to me," ordered the King.

The tailor was brought to the palace with great trepidation on his part and the King said:

"I have heard that you are very strong and brave. As you know there are two giants in my kingdom who rob and terrorise my soldiers. I am asking you to free us from them. Do this and you will marry my daughter."

The young tailor did not dare tell the King that in fact it was only seven flies that he had killed. Furthermore the Princess was so beautiful that he decided to try his fate with the giants because he might have some luck.

"If I marry her I will at last be tailor to the royal household," he thought optimistically.

In due course he came across the giants after walking for several hours. The two enormous ill-doers were taking their afternoon nap under a large oak tree.

"Good grief," thought the tailor to himself. "How huge they are! How on earth will I conquer them?"

And he began to think.

"I've got it!" he said quietly, so as not to wake the giants.

He started collecting fairly large stones. When he had succeeded in filling his bag with stones he was satisfied with himself.

The tailor climbed the tree carefully so as not to make a noise which would wake the giants up and sat on a branch directly above them.

Then he opened the bag and started throwing stones at one of the

giants until he
managed to wake
him up.

"Why are you hitting me?" said the giant who had woken up, to his companion, very annoyed. "You must be mad!" replied the other. "I haven't done anything."
Whereupon they began

fighting with each other furiously whilst the tailor, hiding in the tree, laughed at them.

"Take that, and that!"
they were saying,
punching each other.

And they hit each

other so much that they fell to the ground, worn out. The tailor then climbed down from the tree and, checking that the giants were senseless, celebrated his triumph, shouting:

"I have conquered them. I will be the Princess's husband and the King's tailor."

The tailor took a rope from his bag, tied the giants up soundly and went to the palace in search of soldiers so that the giants could be taken prisoner and put in the royal dungeons.

"What a strong lad he is!" exclaimed the soldiers. "How on earth did he do it?"
The King rewarded the tailor for his heroic achievement when he saw the two giants arrive,

wounded and as his prisoners.

"If I hadn't seen it with my own eyes, I would never have believed it!" he exclaimed. "How did you manage to fight alone with two giants?"

The tailor said nothing so as not to lie.

The wedding was celebrated with much finery and joy the following week. The whole kingdom heaved a sigh of relief, free at last from the menace of the giants and the tailor's fame spread throughout the world.

When the young couple were man and wife the tailor said:

"From now on I shall make all the King's clothes!"

And when the Monarch died, the tailor became King and tailor at the same time!

THE END

SINBAD THE SAILOR

ONCE upon a time there was a poor old man who lugged bags of medicine around with him. One evening he was very tired and sat down outside a palace.

"Poor old me," he

lamented. "I work all day just for a few crumbs, while other people have everything they want without ever having to work for it."

The master of the house heard the beggar's complaints and asked him to come in and sit at his table.

fortune?" he asked.

"I shall tell you my story and then you will know just how much I have suffered. Sit down and take supper with us and listen.

"Do you think that everything I have was given to me by good

When my father died I squandered almost all of my fortune. With the last bit of money he had left me I bought some goods and set out with other merchants to trade in far away countries and to get back everything I had lost.

The voyage went well until we stopped at a small island to rest. We lit a fire but soon noticed that the island was a sleeping whale! The animal awoke, enraged and we were tossed into the water. Some of us managed to reach the ship but I was left to fate in the middle of the sea.

Thanks to luck I managed to grab hold of a barrel and got inside it to avoid being eaten by the sharks.

In any case my situation was desperate since the ship had left without seeing me and I was miles away from any known coastline.

When I had lost all hope of being saved, the tide carried me to a coast which I didn't know. I couldn't see any plants but the whole ground was covered with diamonds as big as your fist.

'Am I to die here, with nothing to eat, but with such riches?' I asked myself.

The sun was suddenly clouded by an enormous bird which was swooping down to pick up a huge chunk of

meat which I had not seen until then. I remembered hearing people talk of an inaccessible valley full of diamonds where lumps of meat were dropped so that huge birds would pick them up with diamonds stuck to them.

I filled my pockets with diamonds and tied myself to another lump of meat which was there, using my turban.

'The bird will carry me from here,' I thought. 'This is my only chance to escape from starvation.'

Then I settled back and waited.

Before long another enormous bird appeared. It grabbed the piece of meat, to which I was attached, in its talons and rose into the air.

Just imagine how frightened I was, flying hundreds of feet above ground! But thanks to God no harm came to me.

Soon we arrived at our destination. The problem now was to escape without the bird seeing me as it could have killed

me with one peck of its beak just as if I were a troublesome fly.

I prayed and begged that the bird would not have a mate waiting for food. Suddenly there was a huge noise. Several men appeared, making so much noise that the bird left, forgetting its load.

'So that is it,' I said to
myself. 'That is how all the
'diamond fishers' get the
food back and separate
the precious stones from
it.'

'What on earth are you doing here?' asked a man, astonished. And I told him about my adventures. 'That is unlucky for me. I spent all my money

buying that lump of meat and, apart from you, I have not got a single diamond in payment,' he said, rather annoyed.

'You haven't lost anything,' I said to him. 'Your food saved my life and as compensation for that I am offering you half of what I managed to get from the valley of diamonds.'

The chap was very happy and thanked me because that little pile of stones was a bigger prize

than he had ever hoped for and he took me home with him to recover from my adventure.

I stayed with him for several weeks, recovering from my terrible adventure and he treated me like a brother, he was so grateful.

However, one day a ship visited which was travelling to Baghdad and I got on it to go home after buying a large amount of goods to trade.

I had this and other dangerous adventures to make my fortune and I have survived everything all right. I have told you about them so that you

will not bemoan your
fate—it could be worse,
you know.''
    Then he generously
gave the beggar some
money and he went away

thanking God for all he
had learned that night.

THE END

THE SELFISH GIANT

THE giant had gone on a trip to visit his friend the ogre and had forgotten to close his garden gate. As soon as the children found out they went to play there. How lovely it was, full of flowers, cheered-up by the birds singing and children's laughter. Every afternoon after school the village children swarmed in.

The trees were very pleased by the children's presence. They were glad to see them enjoying the lovely fruit. The children climbed them and never ceased clambering about, like bees in search of honey. It seemed as if eternal Spring had come to that beautiful spot.

However, after seven years the giant returned. He opened his garden gate and when he saw all

those children playing
there he shouted:
    "What are you doing
here? Who gave you
permission to come here? Get out of here this very
minute."
    You see the giant was very selfish.
    The children fled, terrified.

The giant locked the gate with a big padlock and the children knew that they could never play there again.

The trees and flowers became sad and lost their bright colours, as if the sun no longer fed them. The children had brought joy into their lives and now they would no longer be seeing them.

Months went by and the selfish giant was alone all day, every day.

"Huh," he said. "Why should I let them come into my garden? If they haven't got anywhere to play that's their problem, not mine!"

The children peeped boldly over the garden wall but the giant frightened them away immediately.

Autumn arrived. The wind swept the dead leaves along and the garden became a sad place. The selfish giant said to himself:

"Oh I hope the fine weather will come soon!"

Although he was selfish, he loved the flowers and hated Winter most of all.

Winter came and it snowed for several days. The snow in the village melted, but the snow in the giant's garden stayed and it seemed as if it would never go away.

The giant was freezing cold!

"It is strange how long the Winter is lasting this year," said the giant to himself.

One day the children found a hole in the garden wall and were bold enough to go through it to play. That corner was filled with joy and Spring as soon as they went into it.

The giant saw this from the house and thought to himself:

"I never realized that it

is the children who bring the Spring," and regretted his selfishness.

The giant went up to the children to tell them that they could stay, but when they saw him coming they fled as they were terrified of him.

Only one very small child stayed behind, since as he had his back turned he didn't see the giant coming.

"Why are you crying, little one?" asked the giant, kneeling down to comfort him.

"Because I can't climb this tree on my own," he replied.

He did not appear to be at all afraid of the giant, despite being smaller than his companions.

For the first time in his life the giant felt tenderness.

He picked the child up gently in his huge hands and lifted him up into the tree—he was fascinated. Then the child kissed the giant and the huge fellow felt his heart melting.

The child was clapping his hands with joy. He reached out easily to pick the fruit on the tree. The sun shone its warmest rays on the two people.

"From now on all the children can play in my garden," said the giant.

There was a huge hammer nearby and the giant broke down the wall which was separating the garden from the village, brick by brick.

"I want you children to always be in my orchard and play here," he said. The children were amazed!

Time passed and he never went back on his word. Every afternoon they visited the giant who loved to see them playing. But most of all he liked the child who had kissed him.

"Is your little companion coming?" he would ask.

And the children always replied, "We don't know."

Years went by, with their Springs and Winters, and the giant still looked out for the precious child who had been his first friend. Every day he was growing older and more tired.

One Winter's morning he opened the window and saw that one tree in the garden had come into blossom, despite all the snow. Then he saw the child he loved so dearly standing nearby.

"You've come, at last!" exclaimed the giant. "But what has happened to your hands? How did you hurt them?"

"Don't worry giant," replied the child. "These are the wounds of love and as you let me play in your garden I have come to take you away to mine, which is paradise. Will you come with me?"

"Of course I will," said the giant.

The next day the children found the giant lying on the grass as if he were sleeping, but they knew he had died.

They never saw the little child who had captured the giant's heart ever again. But the children of those children still play in the garden every day, and they know this story.

THE END

SNOW WHITE AND ROSE RED

IN a pretty little house near a wood there lived a widow with her two daughters. One was as white as the icing on a cake and was called Snow White. The other was always as red as a rose and was called Rose Red. The two girls were very

kind and domesticated.

"Nothing will ever separate us, mother," they always said, since they loved each other very much.

Every day, after helping their mother in the vegetable garden, they went to play in the nearby wood. The little animals came to know them and were not afraid of them. The birds, deer and squirrels let the girls stroke them and they played with them happily in the grass.

One Winter's evening there was a terrible snow storm. Suddenly there was a knock at the door and Snow White went to open it. An enormous bear appeared in the doorway and the children let out a shriek.

"Please let me in, I'm very cold," said the bear.

"Come in, my friend," replied the mother. "Come inside and get warm."

The bear lay down
near the fire.

"Brush all the snow off
his coat," their mother
told them.

At first the children did
what they were told
rather timidly, but soon
gained confidence when
they saw he was gentle
and they were soon
playing with him.

"Hey, you're tickling
me," he laughed.

The bear stayed at their house throughout the Winter. He played with the two girls, listened to the mother's stories until late and then slept throughout the night.

Snow White and Rose Red got so used to him that they loved him like their best friend.

However, Spring arrived and one morning the bear said to them:

"I must go back to the mountains now and guard my treasure from the greedy dwarfs. I shan't be returning until next Winter, my dears."

Snow White and Rose Red kissed him several times and made him promise not to forget them.

Several weeks passed and Summer arrived. The two sisters were out walking one day when they met a tiny man who was struggling desperately and jumping up and down as he had tangled his beard in some hawthorn.

"What are you staring at, silly youngsters?" he cried. "Help me to get free!"

They tried to untangle the beard but as they couldn't, Rose Red took a pair of scissors from her pocket and cut off the tuft of beard which was entangled so as to free him.

"Now look what you've done, stupid," he grunted, very annoyed. "See, you've cut off my beard."

And off he ran without even thanking them.

The next day they were walking by a river when they met another dwarf in trouble. A fish was tugging at his beard and was on the point of dragging him into the water.

"Help, help," cried the little man. "Free me from this monster!"

The girls grabbed the dwarf by the feet and tugged.

However, the fish was so big and strong that there was no choice but to cut off his beard to free him from the creature.

"That's a fine thing you've done," protested the dwarf, "leaving me without a beard."

Again he left without so much as a thank you.

A few days later they had gone a little way from the house when they heard cries of help yet again.

"Help, help! This terrible bird is carrying me away!"

An eagle had grabbed the little man by the beard and was about to carry him up into the air. The children seized him by the trousers but the eagle held on so strongly

that they had to cut off his beard to free him.

As soon as he was freed the dwarf growled:

"What a clumsy pair you are! I'm going somewhere else with my jewels."

He had a bag of precious stones at his feet which the children had not seen until then.

"Can we see them?" they asked.

"Oh no, you'll be trying to steal them from me next," replied the dwarf.

Suddenly an enormous
bear appeared, roaring
furiously:

"Give me back my
jewels, thieving dwarf, or
I will kill you!"

"Please don't kill me,"
begged the dwarf. "The
children stole them, not
me."

The dwarf was lying,
but the children who
were very frightened fled.

The bear started chasing them.
"Eh, stop. I'm not going to hurt you," he shouted.
When she heard that voice, Snow White thought:
"Isn't that the voice of our friend the bear? If I'm

wrong and stop the animal will surely kill me. If I'm
right and he is our bear and I don't stop, he will be
very sad. I'll trust in luck and stop."

So Snow White stopped and was so surprised when she saw the bear changing into a fine Prince who said to her:

"Thank you for trusting me, Snow White. Your

kindness has saved me from the terrible spell which changed me into a bear."

Rose Red joined them and they all hugged each other.

Snow White married the Prince and Rose Red married one of his brothers, who was just as fine and elegant as he.

"We shall never be separated," repeated the sisters on the day of their royal wedding.

And from that day on they all lived happily ever after.

THE END

CONTENTS